William Kotzwinkle, Glenn Murray, and Elizabeth Gundy

Rough Weather Ahead for Walter the Farting Dog

Illustrated by **Audrey Colman**

PUFFIN BOOKS

PUFFIN BOOKS

Published by the Penguin Group

Penguin Young Readers Group, 345 Hudson Street, New York, New York 10014, U.S.A.

Penguin Group (Canada), 90 Eglinton Avenue East, Suite 700, Toronto, Ontario, Canada M4P 2Y3

(a division of Pearson Penguin Canada Inc.)

Penguin Books Ltd, 80 Strand, London WC2R ORL, England

Penguin Ireland, 25 St Stephen's Green, Dublin 2, Ireland (a division of Penguin Books Ltd)

Penguin Group (Australia), 250 Camberwell Road, Camberwell, Victoria 3124, Australia

(a division of Pearson Australia Group Pty Ltd)

Penguin Books India Pvt Ltd, 11 Community Centre, Panchsheel Park, New Delhi - 110 017, India

Penguin Group (NZ), cnr Airborne and Rosedale Roads, Albany, Auckland 1310, New Zealand

(a division of Pearson New Zealand Ltd)

Penguin Books (South Africa) (Pty) Ltd, 24 Sturdee Avenue, Rosebank, Johannesburg 2196, South Africa

Registered Offices: Penguin Books Ltd, 80 Strand, London WC2R ORL, England

First published in the United States of America by Dutton Children's Books,
a division of Penguin Young Readers Group, 2005
Published by Puffin Books, a division of Penguin Young Readers Group, 2007

1 3 5 7 9 10 8 6 4 2

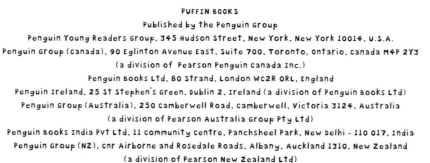
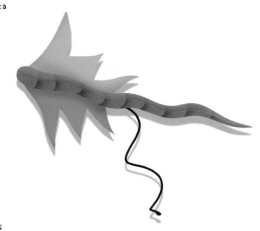

Text copyright © William Kotzwinkle, Glenn Murray, and Elizabeth Gundy, 2005
Illustrations copyright © Audrey Colman, 2005
All rights reserved.

THE LIBRARY OF CONGRESS HAS CATALOGED THE DUTTON CHILDREN'S BOOKS EDITION AS FOLLOWS:
Kotzwinkle, William.
Rough weather ahead for Walter the farting dog / William Kotzwinkle, Glenn Murray,
and Elizabeth Gundy ; illustrated by Audrey Colman.—1st ed.
p. cm.
Summary: When an expert on animal gas tries to cure Walter, his farts keep building up until he floats
away and is blown by the wind to a distant place, where he once again proves himself a hero.
ISBN: 0-525-47218-5 (hc)
[1. Dogs—Fiction. 2. Flatulence—Fiction.]
I. Murray, Glenn. II. Colman, Audrey, ill. III. Title.
PZ7.K855Ro 2005 [E]—dc22 2004056180

Puffin Books ISBN 978-0-14-240845-2

Manufactured in China

Designed by Jason Henry

For everyone who's ever felt
misjudged or misunderstood

Professor Kompressor knocked on the door.
"I understand your dog has a farting disorder."
"It's not a disorder," said Betty and Billy.
"Yes, it is!" shouted Father. "Come on in."

Professor Kompressor said, "I've made a lifelong study of animal gas."

He examined Walter, gently poking around his stomach.

"You'd better be careful," said Father. "He farts when you do that."

"He won't fart at me, will you, Walter?"

Walter farted. Professor Kompressor staggered backward, waving his gas meter. "Ten-point-seven! The highest I've ever recorded. What a remarkable animal."

Walter was pleased to be called remarkable. He liked Professor Kompressor and licked his hand.

"You're a good dog, Walter," said Professor Kompressor, "and I'm going to help you."

He poked around some more. "It's his digestion that causes such powerful farts."

"We don't mind," said Betty and Billy.

"Yes, we do," said Mother.

"Years of research have led me to this special formula," said Professor Kompressor. Powders and potions appeared from his pockets. He plugged in a gleaming machine. "Mix it in my Kompressatron and serve it fresh three times a day."

"We're so grateful," said Mother.

So three times a day, Mother mixed the special formula in the Kompressatron.

"His farts aren't as bad," said Billy hopefully.

"They're worse than ever," said Father.

"Your father is right," said Mother.

That night Father decided to mix the formula himself. He examined the powders carefully. "More of *this*," he decided. "Less of *this* and a *lot* more of that."

Father sniffed the new mixture and smiled. "That's better."

Tastes pretty good, said Walter to himself, and ate it faithfully every day.

"It's working!" cried Mother. "The air smells so fresh."

"Hurray!" said Betty.

Walter was pleased, too. Everyone was smiling. No one ran away when he came in the room. Father even hugged him.

However, inside Walter, gas was building up slowly.

"That dog's getting fat," said Father.

But it wasn't fat.

It was farts, waiting to be set free.

Professor Kompressor's mixture and Father's expert touch were turning Walter into a blimp.

Walter began taking strange little bounces when he walked across the room.

One evening he floated over Father's chair.

"Great jump, Walter," said Billy.

But it wasn't a jump. It was gas.

The following evening, Billy and Betty were in their room doing homework.

"Billy," said Betty, "look outside!"

Betty and Billy raced out of the house.

Walter was floating over the trees.

"Walter, come down!" cried Betty.

But Walter couldn't come down.

He floated on into town.
Quite a view, he said to himself.

A breeze came up and blew him over to the other end of town.
This is getting serious, said Walter.

He knew the problem was gas. He knew the solution was farting.

He squeezed.

He pressed his belly with his paws.

He twisted into a knot.

Nothing.

He floated all night long. When morning came, he was high above the world.

"Mommy," said a little girl, "look at the balloon."

"It's lost," said the little girl's mother. "It will never come back."

Walter floated for days. He floated over green hills and blue rivers. He floated over skyscrapers and farms. He floated in the dark and the rain.

He felt lonely and cold.

He went whichever way the wind carried him.

Suddenly the wind grew much stronger, and he wasn't alone any longer.

The air around him was filled with the flutter of tiny, frozen wings.

Millions of butterflies were caught in a freezing windstorm. They had been on their way to their winter home when the storm took them by surprise.

Poor butterflies, said Walter to himself.

The wind was driving them down toward the frozen lake below.

I've got to help them, thought Walter.

He knew he had it in him, if he could just get it out. He grunted. He groaned. He pressed.

He looked into their tiny insect faces. It was now or never.

He let it rip.
A blast of warm gas lifted the butterflies out of their dive.
It melted the ice on their wings. It carried them to the far side
of a mountain, where the sun was shining.

They touched down in a field of wildflowers.
A forest ranger in his tower grabbed his two-way radio.
"I think those butterflies are going to be okay."

Out of gas, Walter went down like a rocket.

He splashed into a pond and doggy-paddled to the shore.

He shook himself dry. Then he sniffed the air, turned around, and started the long walk home.

He'd gone only a little way when the ranger pulled up in his Jeep. "Can I give you a lift, Wonder Dog?"

"Somebody sent us a big package," said Mother,
looking out the window.
  "It's not a package!" cried Billy. "It's Walter!"
  "See," said Father, "I told you he'd find his way home."
  "Oh Walter," said Betty, "we're so glad you're back."
  "Not half as glad as we are," said the deliverymen.